THE
PRAIRIE SCHOONERS

THE
PRAIRIE SCHOONERS

WRITTEN AND ILLUSTRATED BY
GLEN ROUNDS

HOLIDAY HOUSE • NEW YORK

Contents

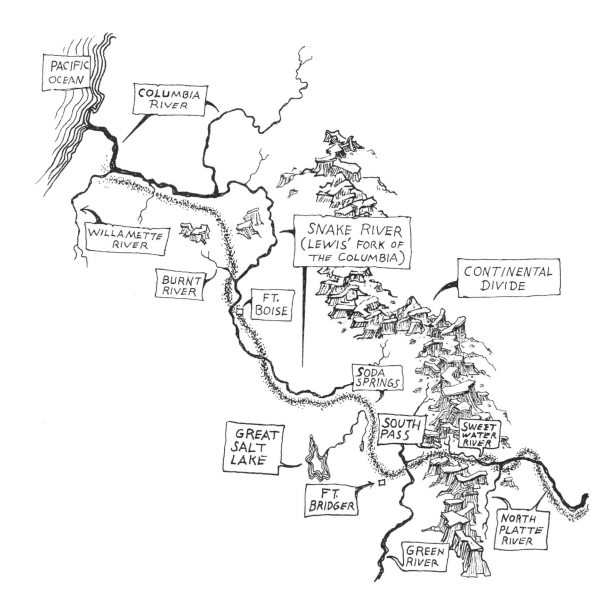

THE OREGON TRAIL
ROUTE OF THE
PRAIRIE SCHOONERS
1843-1868

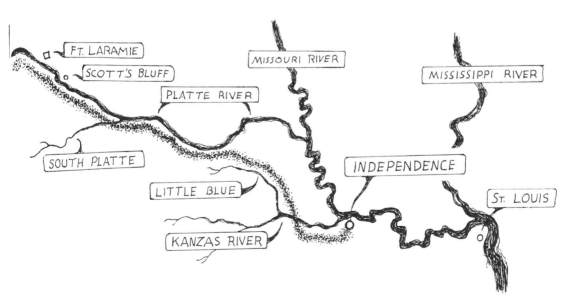

CHAPTER ONE

The

Oregon Trail

In the summer of 1843 the first train of Prairie Schooners successfully made the two thousand-mile trip from Independence, Missouri, to the Oregon Territory and settled an issue of nearly forty years standing. For Government interest in the settlement of the area explored by Lewis and Clark in 1805 and 1806 had been slow to develop.

In 1819 the United States bought Spain's title to what later became Oregon, Washington, and Idaho —but mostly because that land came in a package deal with the purchase of Florida. In 1820 a Virginia congressman, John Floyd, suggested setting up a territorial government and authorizing settlement there, but found almost no support for his idea.

From the Missouri River east to the Atlantic, fleets of river steamboats and a growing network of railroads were already providing reliable transportation for goods and people. And travelers by stagecoach or wagon found passable roads almost everywhere, with streams bridged and taverns and small settlements scattered at convenient intervals along the way.

But to the west, the existing maps of the region separating the Missouri River and the tributaries of the Columbia showed nearly two thousand miles of barren desert, rugged mountains, and powerful tribes of warlike Indians. So there was a widely held belief that this wilderness would forever be an impassable

barrier to both trade and settlement, and that the westward expansion of the country would end at the edge of the Great Plains.

But, unimpressed by the opinions of the politicians, the trappers and fur traders continued to probe and explore that wild country for their own purposes. Soon they were making regular trips between the Missouri and the Columbia River country, and the existence of the South Pass as a gateway to the western slopes of the Rockies became common knowledge.

In 1828 Jedediah S. Smith led the first overland expedition by white men west from the Missouri to

California. Before returning the following year he traveled as far south as San Diego, then turned north to reach the Columbia in the Oregon country.

In 1830, to prove that a road to the Northwest was practical, Smith led a party of loaded wagons across the plains to the Rocky Mountains. Following the fur traders' route up the Platte and the Sweetwater the wagons successfully made the trip almost to the Continental Divide and the entrance to South Pass before finally turning back. But returning to his starting point after having been gone six months, Smith found that the country at large remained unimpressed, and his exploit went almost unnoticed.

But in 1834 a small party of missionaries under the leadership of Marcus Whitman, carrying their goods on pack animals and following the fur traders' route through South Pass, made their way to Oregon and

established a mission on the Willamette River. Two years later Whitman, making his second trip to the missionary settlement, took one wagon along with his pack train. It broke down and had to be abandoned at Ft. Boise on the Snake River, but that was nearly a thousand miles farther into the wilderness than any wheel had gone before.

During the next few years the tales told by the fur company men and the returning missionaries—tales of rich soil and a good climate—began to circulate widely in the East and to catch the imagination of the always land-hungry people. More and more pressure was put on Congress to establish a territorial government in Oregon and to authorize American settlement there. Finally, in 1843, such a bill was put before Congress—and without waiting to see whether or not it passed, an expedition called "The Great Oregon Migration" was organized.

This first emigrant group, setting out to follow the route of the missionaries and the fur trappers, consisted of nearly a thousand people—men, women, and children—a hundred and twenty wagons, and

nearly five thousand head of cattle, horses, mules, and other livestock. Traveling in a single body, well-equipped and organized under a semimilitary system of elected captains and subcaptains, they left Independence for the Platte late in May. Marcus Whitman, making his third trip to the Northwest, traveled with them, and his knowledge of the route probably contributed to the successful overcoming of the hazards of the experiment. In any event, the expedition reached the valley of the Willamette late in October,

having lost only seven members to accident or sick-
ness on the way.

In 1844 a party of nearly fourteen hundred people, also traveling in a single train, followed the
tracks of the earlier party led by Whitman the year
before. They were delayed by bad weather and accidents but eventually reached Oregon late in the
season.

By then the Oregon Trail was an established fact,
and "Oregon Fever" swept the East. In the summer
of 1845 nearly three thousand people crossed the
Missouri to seek their fortunes in the Northwest, and
more followed each year. And for the next few years
the white-topped wagons—"the Prairie Schooners"
—in groups of fifty to a hundred swarmed along the
Trail during the summer months in almost endless
lines.

And the covered wagon did for the settlement of
the Northwest—and later of California—what the
wooden sailing ships had done for the New World,
and the steamboats and railroads for the Ohio and
Mississippi valleys.

CHAPTER TWO

The

Prairie Schooners

The wagons carrying the emigrants and their goods were of many kinds and sizes—of all ages and in various states of repair. There were lightly built outfits from the flat farming states, huge high-sided Conestogas built for hauling freight in the Eastern mountains, and every size in between. There was even an occasional two-wheeled cart or top buggy to be seen among them. Some were drawn by strings of six or eight pairs of horses or oxen, while others were hitched to a single team.

The size and condition of his outfit depended on

what the emigrant, in his ignorance of the road ahead, thought was suitable—or what he could afford. But big wagons, middle-sized wagons, small wagons, or two-wheeled carts—all had canvas wagon covers stretched over wooden bows to protect their loads.

It was from their resemblance to small ships when seen from a distance, pitching and swaying across the wide plains with their white canvas tops ballooning and whipping in the wind, that they came, naturally enough, to be called Prairie Schooners.

And the emigrants, fitting out their wagons for the long trip to Oregon, faced much the same problems as sailors readying small ships for a long voyage into unknown seas.

From the Missouri westward to Oregon the settlers faced a voyage of a hundred to a hundred and fifty days across an unknown and uninhabited land.

The first five hundred miles was a sea of rolling plains rising steadily to the foot of the Rocky Mountains and crossed by sluggish, treacherous rivers. Beyond that were more weeks of travel over high mountain passes, through deep rocky gorges, and across wide, barren deserts.

And for the entire trip a wagon train would of necessity be as self-contained as a fleet of wooden sailing ships at sea. With the exception of a few forts and trading posts maintained for the fur trappers there would be no place to put in for repairs, to replenish supplies, or to make good any oversight in equipment.

Not only must the emigrants find room in the wagons for their clothing and household goods, but also for supplies enough for the entire trip, with allowance made as well for delays due to accident, bad weather, and a hundred other possibilities. And all

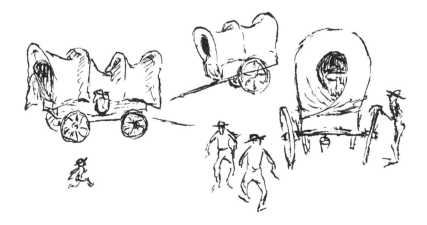

these things had to share the limited space with the ploughs, shovels, axes, seed grain, and other items that would be needed for the clearing and cultivating of the new farms in the wilderness.

Nor was that all, for the months of jolting travel over the rough trail would take a heavy toll of even the strongest wagons and equipment. Axles would break, and iron tires would work loose from wheels shrunken by long spells of dry weather and have to be cut and shortened. Wooden spokes and felloes would splinter and have to be replaced by others made on the spot. Chains and ox yokes would break or be lost, and always there would be sore-footed oxen and horses needing new iron shoes to save them from permanent laming.

So to the constantly growing loads would be added tools for rough blacksmithing, carpentry, and wagon building, along with nails, rivets, rods, and strap iron

for making horseshoes, ox shoes, or wagon hardware. And water barrels, lashed to the outsides of the wagons, were a necessity that must not be overlooked. Everything had to be provided for—even the lack of so small an item as horseshoe nails could mean disaster in certain circumstances.

Not every wagon carried the full list of these items, of course, but careful leaders made sure before setting out that somewhere in the train these necessary things could be found when needed. And any man with experience as a blacksmith or wheelwright was a welcome addition to any such organization.

And like sailors exploring strange lands, the emigrants had to be prepared to defend themselves from possible attack by hostile natives, so guns and ammunition were included in the lists of necessary supplies. Nowhere would there be anyone to call on for help in the event of accident or attack.

CHAPTER THREE

The

Prairie Port

During the years of the Oregon migration, Independence, Missouri, the main jump-off point for the West, was a busy two-sided port. Along the river-front the steamboats from Saint Louis and the East unloaded goods and emigrants and their possessions, while on the prairie side were all the facilities for fitting out and supplying the Prairie Schooners for the land voyage across the plains and mountains. Most of the emigrants had brought their wagons and live-stock with them from the East, but there were last-minute supplies and additional equipment to buy. Wagons were strengthened, repaired, or traded off for others larger and stronger. Men driving horse teams traded them for oxen and ox gear or bought additional teams to take care of growing loads or to replace stock lost to disease or accident.

Others with dangerously ramshackle wagons and poor stock were advised to buy better equipment before attempting the trip.

So in every street the wagon-makers, wheelwrights, harness-makers, blacksmiths, gunsmiths, and merchants were busy at their trades. Stocks were cleared from their shelves almost as fast as replacements could be unloaded from the steamboats jamming the riverfront. From pens within the town and from herds held out on the prairie the dealers in horses, mules, and oxen bought, sold, and traded from daylight far into the night.

There was a brisk demand for livestock and equipment of every kind, and, as is always the case where buyers outnumber sellers, the prices asked had little relation to the actual value of the item for sale. No guarantees were given, and experienced buyers carefully examined every animal offered and went over wagons and other gear inch-by-inch to find hidden defects before settling down to whittle and haggle over prices.

But a little ginger, properly applied, can do wonders toward the rejuvenating of an aged horse or ox, while lampblack and lard and other horsetraders' mixtures were equally effective at hiding otherwise obvious blemishes. Paint, shipped by steamboat from the East, was expensive. But the small amount needed to make a split wheel spoke or wagon tongue look strong and solid was considered a good investment by the traders.

So it was not uncommon for a man to pay a hugely inflated price for animals that later proved to be diseased or otherwise unfit, or to buy what appeared to be a splendid bargain in a wagon only to have it

break down before it had been on the trail a week. The sellers of poor draft animals and rickety wagons moved from spot to spot—and even if they were found, a complaint, unless it could be backed up by force, was worse than useless. Traveler's checks and credit cards had not been invented yet, so the emigrant's bank was his pants pocket, and out and out robbery was not uncommon.

So before the emigrants even set out, many found themselves without money to equip themselves and had to turn back.

In spite of all this the preparations went on day after day. Bacon, flour, sugar, gunpowder, lead, clothing, boots, and a hundred other items were added to the growing stacks of supplies piled around the emigrant camps outside of town.

Space somehow had to be found in the wagons
for sacks, boxes, tools, furniture, bedding, clothes,
and food. The heavier items went in first with lighter
things on top. Although some of the emigrants carried tents, more often the women and girls slept and
dressed inside the wagons under the canvas, so the
loads had to be arranged to leave level space for beds
on top of at least a part of the load. And often a firm
foundation had to be made for a rocking chair, to be
used as a perch for somebody's grandmother during
the long days of travel.

Food boxes and cooking utensils that would be
in daily use had to be stowed where they could be
easily reached when needed. Occasionally a family
lucky enough to have more than the usual resources
would own two or more wagons, which eased the

problem somewhat. Some even had space enough for a small stove and could cook inside their wagons during bad weather.

But more often, when the last bit of space in the wagons had been filled, there were absolutely essential items still lying on the ground. Then everything would have to be unloaded again while families quarreled and bickered over the question of what could possibly be left behind and what simply must be taken.

Separating women from their household possessions is not an easy thing. But a wagon box would hold only so much, and before long the campgrounds were surrounded by an ever increasing litter of furniture, trunks, crockery, and other things discarded to make room for more urgently needed items. Newcomers from the East wandered among these abandoned treasures, occasionally hauling some especially

attractive bit of furniture to their own wagons. But soon they too were adding their bits to the growing piles of ownerless equipment.

Even with all this activity—the buying and selling, the repairing and trading, the making and remaking of essential lists, and the loading and unloading of the wagons—the over-all impression was of men talking. In twos, fours, tens, and dozens—in the streets, around the blacksmith shops and stock pens, on the open prairie and in open spaces between the camps—they gathered, talking.

Before setting out on this dangerous voyage into unknown country they were eager for every small scrap of information about the trail and the problems they'd have to face. Men who had spoken to someone who had once made the trip shared their small fund of information with those less fortunate. There were endless discussions of the merits of vari-

ous types of wagons, of the advantages and disadvantages of oxen as compared to horses and mules. There were conflicting details concerning camping places and the best river crossings, rumors of Indian uprisings, and a thousand other things to be discussed and evaluated.

So day after day, while glum, red-eyed women retrieved odd treasures from the pile discarded on the plain and tried to hide them in the already overloaded wagons, the men talked.

Men who had no knowledge of the trail manufactured it—some innocently, as people will, simply to avoid admitting ignorance on an important subject, and others with malice, in order to foist off on some innocent emigrant some item of equipment that in spite of its great cost would later prove to be worthless, or worse. Other enterprising fellows who had been over the trail—and some who hadn't—

peddled impressively printed "Trail Guides" listing camping places, the best river crossings, landmarks, cutoffs, information concerning the best methods of dealing with Indians, and other bits of trail lore guaranteed to be of value to the greenhorn. These naturally found a ready sale, and while some proved to be valuable aids, the greater share served only to enrich the compiler and confuse the emigrants.

But as the season advanced, with the ground beginning to dry and new grass showing on the plains, family after family hitched up, leaving Independence for Council Groves a few miles nearer the edge of the plains. It was here, in another huge sprawling camp, that the wagon trains were organized for the long trip.

For protection from the Indians and for mutual assistance, the emigrants would travel in groups of

GUIDES
TO THE
OREGON
TRAIL

LISTING:
CAMPGROUNDS
RIVER CROSSINGS
SHORT CUTS:
ALSO
VALUABLE HINTS
AND INFORMATION

twenty to a hundred wagons. These trains were made up in various ways. Men who either had made the trip before or had hired a guide who knew the trail often were willing to let other families join them for a fee, providing they agreed to abide by rules set out beforehand. Others who had been neighbors in the East or who had been drawn together by any of a dozen other reasons, formed trains of their own.

The makeup of any such group posed many problems that took careful consideration. Its members would be thrown together for months on the road under the most difficult conditions, and the safety of all depended in some measure on the reliability and dependability of each individual. Once they got started none could be left behind, and one weak, overloaded team or broken-down wagon could delay and endanger an entire train. Also, too large a percentage of families with more women and children

than strong men was a thing to avoid, for not only would it be necessary to have a large number of armed men available in the event of Indian attack, but brawn would be needed to get the wagons through many of the difficulties facing them on the trail.

Groups formed and later dissolved again. Weak, improvident men tried to join their ill-equipped wagons to the trains of stronger, better-equipped leaders, and often were turned away. Others, on the basis of loud talk, apparent knowledge, and an urge for prominence built themselves followings that later might break up and disappear when bickering and doubts set in.

But little by little the trains did form, and there was a continual shifting on the campground as families moved their wagons from one group to camp closer to another they hoped to join. Leaders were elected, rules and bylaws proposed and adopted or discarded according to the tempers of the people. And nearly every morning one or more strings of wagons would pull away from the campground and set out across the plain in the direction of the Platte.

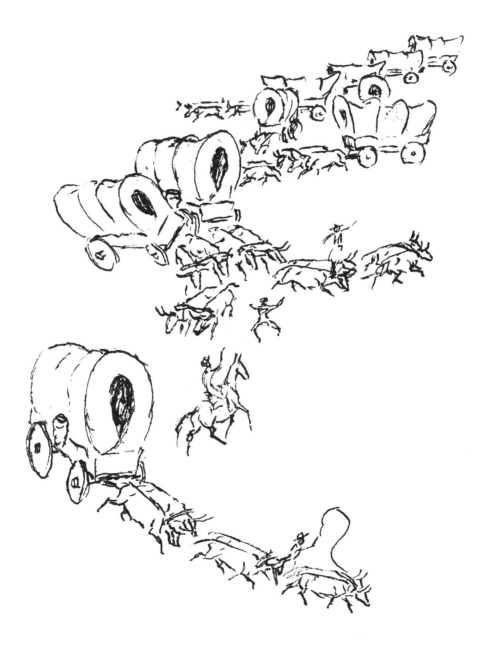

CHAPTER FOUR

First Day

on the Trail

Getting a wagon train lined up and ready to start the first day's travel was not the simple matter one might think. The emigrants would have been up and stirring their cookfires at the first light, all with the best intentions of making an early start. But almost as soon as breakfast was over things would begin to go wrong.

Someone was almost sure to discover that an ox —if not more than one—had wandered off, and hitching would have to be delayed until the creature was found and brought back. Elsewhere a half-trained animal, resenting the feel of the unfamiliar yoke on his neck, would break loose and create a great confusion among the wagons, scattering women and children and upsetting cookpots and grub boxes until he was finally cornered.

Cattle tend to be somewhat conservative, and an ox finding himself being yoked to a complete stranger might set up a diversion of his own—tangling chains and threatening to overturn the wagon during his violent objections.

Yokes and other gear were misplaced or discovered to be missing some essential pin or ring. And all through the camp cattle bawled and men shouted and waved their arms, while boys and barking dogs were underfoot everywhere.

Any of the experienced freighters passing on the nearby Santa Fe Trail could have straightened out the confusion in short order. But among any such

group of emigrants there was usually no more than
a scattering of men who really understood dealing
with rebellious livestock and complicated gear. These
few were constantly being called from their own outfits to take charge of one emergency or another
among the less experienced.

So, what with one thing and another, it was usually
well into the forenoon before the teams were finally
hitched and ready to begin pulling the wagons into
line. Even then the delays were not yet over. At the
last minute some family was sure to have lost a dog,
or have a child who had wandered away, or a smaller
one who was still on his pot and refused to be hurried. Somewhere else a woman still unhandy with
this sort of camp life would find she'd neglected to
take the last kettle of beans off the fire to cool and
was now faced with the problem of what to do with it.

But sooner or later everybody would at last be
ready, with the wagons roughly pointed in the direc-

tion of the Trail. But the picture of the white-hatted wagon boss standing in his stirrups to give the Cavalry "Forward" signal while crying "Wagons, Ho!" was seldom, if ever, seen in real life. As a general thing the lead driver waited until everybody down the line seemed to be ready, then whacked the nearest ox with his whip and hollered "Git!" or something like it. The next driver waited a proper interval and did the same—and so it went down the line until every wagon was moving.

Once under way such a wagon train made a handsome sight. The long line of white-topped prairie schooners strung out for a mile or two across the plain, rocking slowly over the rough ground while on either side of the trail were small bunches of loose stock—oxen, milch cows, horses, mules, and even sheep—herded by boys and older girls, or men working their way to the new country.

From their starting place to the first night's camp was a matter of only a few miles, but almost before they were off the old campground they began to encounter samples of the mishaps and delays that would plague them for the next few months.

The first trouble usually came to the herders of the loose stock. A headstrong old cow, not liking the looks of the trail ahead, might suddenly curl her tail and break back with the idea of rejoining the herds she could still hear bawling on the old campground. And by the time she had been headed off and brought back, a dozen others might be lumbering across country in as many different directions.

While the herders ran here and there, dealing with these emergencies, the teamsters were having their own difficulties. Most of the wagons were drawn by two to four pairs of oxen, the yokes of all but the last pair being hooked at intervals along a chain. The teamster walked to the left and a little behind the lead team, guiding it to right or left by shouts of "Gee!" and "Haw!" accompanied by appropriate whacks from his bullwhip. But the sharpness of the turn depended not only on the ideas of the oxen concerned, but on the loudness and authority of the command, so there was room for considerable misunderstanding. Inexperienced teamsters—as many of these folk were—could get into difficulty even with well-trained animals, and many of the teams were anything but reliable. So almost at once the orderly line of wagons began to show lengthening gaps between clusters where trouble had developed.

Confused drivers shouted "Haw!" when they meant "Gee!" cramping the wheels the wrong way while going down a slope, tangling their teams in their chains, and even upsetting their wagons. A command given too soon or too late or too loud or not loud enough could mean the difference between a wagon staying on firm ground or slipping into a gulley.

A driver unused to the plains might decide to take a short cut across a smooth, firm-appearing flat only to suddenly see his oxen floundering helplessly and his wagon mired to the hubs in a boggy spot. Outfits behind him would have to unhitch while the unfortunate greenhorn waded waist deep in the stinking mire, unhitching his own teams and attaching chains to the rear end of his wagon for his neighbors to hitch to. And when his wagon had at last been pulled back to firm ground, often as not his oxen were still trapped. That meant more wading to attach ropes to their horns so they could be pulled out one at a time.

Somewhere else along the line a clumsily lashed water barrel would be jolted loose from its moorings, meaning another delay while it was hoisted back and someone found to show how it should be done.

All these and dozens of similar mishaps dogged all but the most careful emigrants on the first shake-

down leg of their trip. However, since they were still a long distance from Indian country only the nearest wagons stayed behind to help the unfortunates in trouble, while the rest went on. So hour by hour the line of wagons lengthened as stragglers fell farther and farther behind.

Under those circumstances it is not surprising that the first night's camp was often a pretty disorganized affair. The first arrivals, after picking a site, unhitched the teams and took them to water before herding them out to graze. The women, meanwhile, began the unfamiliar job of getting out their supply boxes and starting cookfires, while the children carried water or scoured the neighborhood for fire wood.

Supper was a hurriedly eaten meal, with constant interruption, for the stock had not yet learned road habits and there were frequent alarms as the creatures scattered in this direction and that.

And all the while the outfits that had been delayed on the trail straggled onto the campground in twos and threes, adding to the confusion. Men trying to make camp in the dark drove their wagons over ox yokes and other gear or stumbled into the tent ropes and picket lines of earlier arrivals. Cattle blundered over cookpots and grub boxes set beside dead cook-fires ready for morning and were almost stampeded by the shrill cries and armwaving of indignant women in long white nightgowns.

The unexpertly arranged loads of many of the latecomers had been hopelessly jumbled by the day's jolting, and women rooted hopelessly inside the dark wagons for lost food boxes or tried to arrange bedding while the crying of their hungry and overtired children shortened their already ragged tempers. It could be long past midnight before the last wagon was in place, the last team turned out to graze, and the last pair of muddy boots scraped and set to dry.

It is small wonder that many families changed their minds about making the trip and turned back after the second or third day.

CHAPTER FIVE

Accidents

and Delays

The second morning's start was often only a little less disorganized than the first had been, but after a few days on the trail most of the emigrants settled into a routine and went about their chores with a minimum of confusion.

The women organized their cooking arrangements for better efficiency so that at the night camps the cookfires were burning and the big Dutch ovens heating for the meat and biscuits by the time the teams had been unhitched and watered. And in the mornings they cleaned their cooking utensils, repacked supply boxes, and had everything neatly stowed in the wagons by the time the stock had been driven into the circle to be hitched up.

The animals, too, quickly fell into a road routine. Some still insisted on wandering into hidden thickets or out of sight over low hills in search of better grass, or perhaps adventure. But for the most part they seemed content to graze quietly under the eyes of a couple of herders—stuffing their paunches as full as possible before being brought onto a bedground close to the wagons for the night. And in the mornings a driver usually had only to catch the leader of his team and the others would file quietly to their places on the chain and wait to be yoked.

Some families carried a crate or two of chickens slung underneath their wagons, and even these soon became trailwise. Morning and night, as well as at noon stops, the crate doors would be opened and

the birds would hurry out to join the grazing live-stock. Scratching about in the grass or chasing insects stirred up by the hoofs of the horses and cattle, they fed and exercised until hitching time. But at the first rattle of chains they hurried back to the safety of the crates, the only homes they knew.

As the drivers became more expert at handling the teams strung out on the long chains, quicker to recognize and avoid possible hazards on the trail, and wiser in the ways of heavily loaded wagons in rough country the trains made better progress.

Depending upon the condition of the road, a wagon train tried to cover ten to fifteen miles a day, and under exceptional conditions might stretch that to twenty, even with the slow ox teams. But there was always the possibility of unforseen delays.

A draw or gulley, apparently no different from a dozen others already crossed without difficulty, might

prove to have a miry bottom and be impassable for wagons. Then the entire line would be halted while conferences were held and suggestions made for the solution to the problem. If no other crossing place could be found there might be a half-day delay while men waded about in the mud and water building a causeway of brush and any timber that was available.

The constant jolting over the rough ground strained the wheels and axles of even the strongest wagons, while long days of pulling heavy loads with no feed but the prairie grass tended to weaken both oxen and horses, so breakdowns were frequent. The light wagons never meant for such rough work, or the ones with too many years of hard use and neglect behind them were the first to go. Axles broke, wheels collapsed, and iron tires worked loose or came entirely off. And it was not unusual, even during those first few weeks, for an overworked ox or crow-bait horse to simply lie down and refuse ever to get up again.

A broken wheel or axle could usually be repaired if timber was available, and the iron tires could be shortened. But the loss of an animal could be disastrous to an emigrant who through ignorance or from lack of money owned only the teams he drove. In some cases the load was simply lightened to compensate for the shrinking team; in others, two families in the same difficulty might double up, rearranging the loads to go in one wagon and combining the teams. But in either case it meant another pile of cherished possessions left beside the road when the wagons finally moved on again.

It was during these first weeks that many of the badly equipped or faint-hearted turned back. At the first campground after such a breakdown several

families might discuss the problem and decide to band together for the return to the Missouri while it was still possible. The better-equipped not only encouraged these people in their decision, but helped them make temporary repairs and when necessary gave them supplies for the return trip. Once the party had reached Indian country and the rugged mountains beyond, there could be no turning back, and every delay would increase the danger to all of being caught by early snows.

A lack of road signs caused the emigrants many delays and lost miles on the trail. When the ruts made by hundreds of wagons following one behind the other became too deep for easy passage, the teamsters straddled the old tracks with their wheels to give their teams better footing. When these in

their turn wore deep, still another track was made alongside the others until an old road might show a line of parallel ruts a quarter of a mile wide, like furrows in a long-abandoned field.

Such roads remain visible for years on the plains— in some parts of the West these wide grass-grown scars of old trails can still be faintly seen, even after more than a hundred years—so to follow the route of previous wagon trains should not have been difficult. But for one reason or another, instead of being a single wide road, the trail continually branched and forked—and at each dividing there was the problem of choosing the right arm of the fork.

Conditions on the plains were continually changing, and a turnoff might have been made to find a better river crossing, to avoid a patch of boggy ground, or simply by someone deciding to take a short cut. Such a detour might either rejoin the main trail a few miles farther on or meander across the country without apparent destination, carrying the emigrants miles out of their way. What appeared to be a well-used fork might lead, after a long pull across a dry and barren stretch of country, only to a campground that no longer offered either grass or water.

There were no detailed road maps and even the information in the Trail Guides was often as not undependable, and nearly always out-of-date. So the emigrants learned to send one or two well-mounted men ahead of the train each morning to scout the route and to locate suitable camping places and river crossings.

As party after party made its way up the trail, each with anywhere from a hundred to a thousand head

of horses, mules, oxen, and loose stock, finding grass became more and more of a problem. Between the Kansas and the head of the Blue the emigrants could find good grass by swinging a few miles wide of the main line of travel. But after they reached the Platte and the junction with the trails from St. Joseph and Council Bluffs the way become more narrow and the problem more troublesome. The herds of the earlier outfits soon ate off the grass close by the camp-grounds so that each following group had to herd their stock farther and farther out on the plain. And the emigrants were no more considerate of others using the trail after them than are the slobs today who litter the highways with cans, papers, garbage, and broken bottles. So it was not unusual for sparks from a breakfast fire carelessly left burning to set grass fires that might run for miles, further reducing the amount of available grazing.

Aside from the damage it did to the grazing, how-ever, the prairie fire was not greatly feared by the emigrants. Clouds of smoke gave warning of its ap-proach, so there was usually plenty of time for scouts

to ride ahead and investigate. Often such fires burned on a narrow front and could be avoided by a slight change of course. But at worst the emigrants had only to set fire to the prairie behind them, then when the ground had cooled a little, pull their wagons to safety on the blackened ground. And as a usual thing the grass surrounding the campgrounds was grazed so close it made an effective fire guard, so there was little danger of being taken unawares at night.

Finding fuel for the hundreds of cookfires was another problem for the emigrants, for timber was scarce along the trail. However, this being buffalo country, the plains were dotted with plate-sized flat gray disks of dried buffalo dung, called buffalo chips by the surprisingly prissy plainsmen. Broken into pieces these burned with a slow, smouldering flame, adding a pungent tang to the campground and reddening the watering eyes of the women hovering over the cookpots. At first some of the women objected to using or handling such fuel, but before long expediency won over prejudice and it was not uncommon to see women and girls darting to this side and that along the way to gather the undistinguished material in their aprons. A mother might stand in a jolting wagon, hanging to the top canvas with one hand and pointing with the other while she cried to a child below, "Over there! To your left, there's another one!"

As they were gathered, the buffalo chips were thrown into a canvas sheet slung hammock fashion under the wagon, and it became a matter of pride to be the owner of such a canvas sagging with reserve fuel.

CHAPTER SIX

River Crossings

Crossing a land where the only roads were the tracks worn by other wagons and where bridges did not exist, the Prairie Schooner people found that getting their heavily loaded wagons across the many streams and rivers caused them much trouble and endless delays.

At a few well-established crossings of the larger rivers enterprising fellows with an eye to business had set up ferries to carry people and their wagons across. The livestock, however, had to swim.

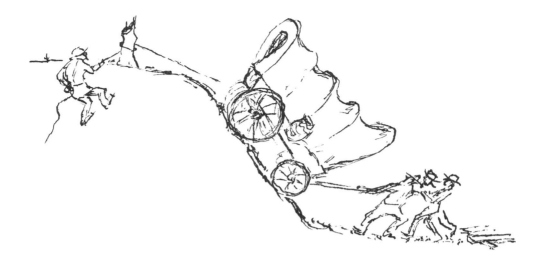

These ferries were crude affairs—often a scow built of cottonwood planks, or a pair of big dugout canoes supporting a platform large enough to carry a wagon. There was seldom time or material for the building of anything but the skimpiest of loading ramps, and frequently the banks were so steep that the wagons had to be let down the slope by ropes and inched carefully onto the unstable platform of the ferry.

Not only was it slow, hard work, but there was always the chance of a slight miscalculation that would result in an upset wagon or a load lost in the water. Unless the stream was unusually wide, the loaded ferry was pulled across by ropes fastened to either bank. And once across, it took more time and

violent effort to get the wagon onto firm ground
again. The water dripping from the hides of the cattle who had swum across soaked the ground at the
water's edge so that hoofs and wheels soon churned
the landing place into a deep loblolly. Brush and
timber thrown down to keep the wagons from sinking in the mud made uncertain and dangerous footing for oxen, so the wagons had to be dragged up the
steep slippery slopes at the ends of long chains
hitched to teams on firm ground above. In the best
of times accidents and upsets were frequent, and in
rainy weather the work was even more difficult.

The four or five men operating a ferry worked from
dawn to dark in the busy season, but by the time one
party had crossed there might be half a dozen long
wagon trains lined up behind, waiting their turn. So
a wait of a week or more for a crossing was not uncommon, and all the while the waiting emigrants
were grazing their stock in wider and wider circles,

making things progressively more difficult for those still to come.

But most of the crossings were made without the help of ferries. As a general thing the plains streams were wide and shallow, with shifting bottoms and quicksand the biggest problems. But having their headwaters far away in the mountains these streams were also subject to sudden flooding from rains far beyond the horizon. So it was not uncommon for a line of prairie schooners creaking across parched prairie—without having seen so much as a cloud for days—to pull down to a crossing and find the river running bank full, with snags and uprooted trees drifting and tumbling in swift, muddy water.

In such a case there was nothing to do but wait for the flood to pass, which might take a day or a week.

If water continued high for several days the impatient emigrants might decide to cross in spite of the

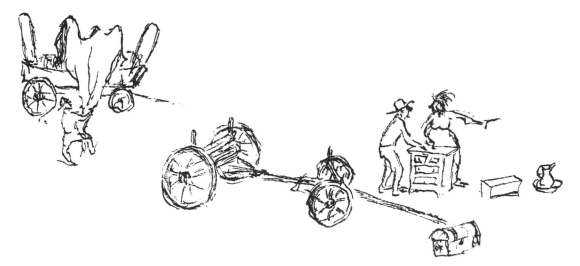

danger. If it was possible to get a rope to the other side, the wagon boxes would be taken off the running gear, the cracks stuffed with rags to make them as watertight as possible, and floated across. These were times of great excitement for the children, but the men hauling the ropes to bring clumsy, makeshift boats across swift current were not so enthusiastic. Nor did the men disassembling the wagons and wrapping the loads in canvas particularly enjoy the wading hip to shoulder deep in the stinking muddy water. But what had to be done they did—for they had a long way to go before snow came.

Grimfaced women pinned up their long skirts and waded about seeing to the safe stowing of their possessions, and when the time came, climbed silently into the flimsy, leaking wagon boxes to be pulled across by the men hauling on the ropes from the other bank.

If everything went well, such a crossing might be

made with nothing worse than some soaked bundles and wet clothing, and perhaps a few head of stock swept away by the water.

But the wagon boxes were unseaworthy craft, and occasionally one was upset by a violent shift in the current or by a drifting log. There were frequently graves on the banks of the streams to remind the emigrants, if they didn't already realize it, that these crossings were dangerous business.

Except in time of flood, however, the crossing was simply a matter of driving into the water on one side and driving out on the other. But most of the plains streams were treacherous and unpredictable, so that even a crossing in regular use was liable to sudden change of temper. Wagon after wagon might have crossed safely, in water no more than hub deep, before a teamster following in the tracks of the one

ahead suddenly found both his oxen and his wagon
sinking in a patch of quicksand or dropping into a
deep hole. In such cases the emigrants, now becom-
ing experienced in such matters, quickly hitched on
additional teams and pulled the outfit to dry ground.

Sometimes firm bottom would be found a few
yards upstream or down, and the rest of the wagons
would cross without difficulty. But just as often the
stirring and trampling would set the entire bottom
to shifting, with patches of quicksand and sudden
dropoffs—invisible under the muddy water—making
the crossing impassable.

So again the wagons would be delayed while men
scouted for miles upstream and down in search of a
new crossing place.

Later, after the emigrants had reached the mountains, the trail often shared narrow gorges with
deep swift streams that often had to be crossed and
recrossed several times in a single day's travel. So it
is not really strange that these people made up no
homesick-sounding songs about the charms of the
Blue, the Platte, the Loup, or the other rivers along
the trail.

CHAPTER SEVEN

Bellyaches

and Broken Bones

Dealing as they did with livestock, heavy wagons, and a violent, inhospitable land the Prairie Schooner people daily faced the risk of broken bones or other injury. A man caught between an unruly ox and a wagon wheel could get ribs broken, or worse. A slip or a moment's inattention while struggling to keep a wagon from overturning on a steep slope could bring another a crushed foot or broken leg. On the trail there was no doctor to call nor ambulance to take the injured to a hospital for treatment.

In the case of a broken leg or arm, whoever had the nerve did his best to pull the limb straight and bind it with rough splints while the neighbors held the patient down.

If the wagon train happened to be near a good camping place they might lay over a day or two, repairing gear and wagons while the victim rested and recovered from the worst effects of shock. But there was always the threat of mountains to be crossed before the snows if the party was to survive, so a place would soon be made for the injured man to lie on bedding piled inside his wagon, and the party would move on. If there was no one in his own family to drive the team, arrangements would be made for someone else to do it. And whether his bones knit or festered the wagons went on, jolting him along mile after mile with nothing except perhaps a little paregoric or one of the many patent cure-alls to ease his pain.

These people were subject to toothache, too, but this was a matter so common that it was taken almost

in stride. If poultices did not reduce the swelling of infected jaws, a pair of pinchers or forceps in the hands of an expert horse shoer would soon remove the trouble.

Deep cuts were not uncommon occurrences, among people careless with knives and axes, and there was an occasional gunshot or arrow wound to be dealt with. Cuts were seldom sewn; depending on the preference of the person doing the repair, the wound would simply be packed with tar, a sulphur and lard mixture, or a mass of spider web, and tightly bound.

Another common way of treating a bad cut, especially if bleeding was difficult to stop, was to pack it with coarse brown sugar before binding. If whiskey happened to be available it was taken internally to deaden the pain rather than as an antiseptic.

This was rough treatment by today's standards,

but in a surprising number of cases the wounds healed quickly and with a minimum of trouble. Of course, scars were usually pretty ragged affairs, and many limbs were left permanently crooked, but in those days such things were to be expected.

Practice of internal medicine was primitive, also. The deep dust of the trail being stirred by the hundreds of wheels and thousands of hoofs was a constant irritant to the people's lungs. Pains in the chest, coughs, and even spitting blood were therefore common complaints. The treatment consisted mostly of poultices and plasters bound on the chest to draw out the poison and the drinking of quarts of herb teas of various kinds to purify the blood.

Much the same was true of bellyaches. The people had never heard of heart attacks, ulcers, appendicitis, and the hundreds of ailments we have today. No matter what the symptoms were or where the distress was centered—high up, low down, or in the middle —it was still a bellyache and there was little to do but dose the patient with purges, herb teas, and patent medicines while hoping for the best.

Being tough people—for in those days the weak and pindling tended to die off early—a surprising number of these folk got well. However, others might continue to ail, making the trip as best they could stretched out in a wagon. But if someone became too ill to be moved, several families might stay behind to wait for improvement or death before hurrying to catch up with the others who had gone on ahead. Graves of both adults and children were more or less common sights along the trail. Some were identified by wooden headboards with a name and date carved or burned into one surface. But in the end the markers would be knocked down by passing Indians or the trampling of buffalo herds. The piece of gray and weathered wood might be picked up to furnish fuel for some later emigrant's cook fire. Even now, one occasionally comes across all that is left of one of those lonely burials—a narrow depression in the grass that can only be seen in certain lights.

Fortunately the ailments of these people were seldom contagious. Traveling as they did in tightly knit groups, and having little contact with any others, they were more or less in constant quarantine. But the harsh diet, dust, the chill of wet clothes and bedding—to say nothing of the constant jolting of the wagons—set up irritations and rheumatisms and a dozen other indefinable ailments.

The hard water of the plains also caused the emigrants much internal discomfort and unease. Sluggish streams and stagnant ponds might be foul, but since the pollution was not of human origin, typhoid

was rare on the trail. But much of the water the people found contained high percentages of dissolved minerals of various kinds, especially salt, sulphur, and alkali in combinations that varied from place to place. Water strong in alkali is a great loosener of bowels, while sulphur water has a nauseating bad-egg smell and a worse flavor.

The human system is amazingly adaptable, adjusting to all sorts of strange conditions if given time. But on the trail the travelers might be drinking alkali water on one day, on the next, sulphur, while on the third the water barrels would be filled from small ponds trampled and fouled by herds of buffalo. It was small wonder that the people's internal workings became irritable and rebellious.

This made things especially difficult for small children. Except for an occasional family no one had milch cows along, and those few soon went dry on the trail. In that day there was no canned or powdered milk, so a child that had been weaned had to do the best he could on water or on coffee, and that was that.

CHAPTER EIGHT

Indians

and Wild Game

As the wagons moved westward into Indian country, the emigrants at first kept their weapons close at hand, and a sharp watch on the country on either side of the trail. Men were warned not to go out of sight of the trail except in the case of necessity, and then only in parties of two or more. And for a while the night guards were nervous and alert. But after a time, if they'd seen no hostile signs, they would again become careless.

Contrary to the impression given by old prints and fiction of the time, the picture of a wagon train drawn up into a circle while the emigrants did battle with thousands of mounted Indians was somewhat overdrawn. There were such occasions, of course—and there are records of an occasional party suffering heavy loss of life or being entirely wiped out and their wagons burned. But these were scattered happenings, and considering the thousands that went over the trail each year the percentage who fought such pitched battles was small.

Nonetheless, Indians were a very real hazard, but usually in less picturesque and violent ways. A small party, usually young braves bent on thievery or harassment, might follow a wagon train for days without ever being seen by the emigrants. Then some man ill-advisedly riding alone out of sight of the wagons might suddenly find Indians on all sides of him. Sometimes such a meeting had fatal consequences for the emigrant, but often as not the Indians would simply steal his horse, gun, and clothes, and maybe

beat him about a little with their lances before leaving him to find his way back to the wagons.

Even when their intentions were reasonably peaceful, the Indians were always on the lookout for a chance to steal cattle or horses, so at noon-camps the oxen were unhitched from the long chains and turned out with their yokes still in place to graze near the wagons where they could be closely watched. At night all the stock was herded loosely until just before dark, then brought back and closely bunched near the wagons. Guards taking two-hour-turns were supposed to watch them through the night, but after a long day on the trail it was not unusual for a newly roused guard to simply take a look about, decide everything was secure and roll himself in his blanket again to continue his sleep.

Often enough this practice brought no unfortunate results, but on the other hand, hitching time

might find several animals missing and plain trails in
the wet grass to show where one or more Indians had
come close to the herd and driven off the stragglers.
A party of mounted men would then have to ride out
to recover the stolen property. If the missing creatures
were oxen they could usually be overtaken in an hour
or two, and unless the Indians were part of a war
party they didn't usually stop to argue, simply aban-
doning any of the animals they'd not already butch-
ered and riding off. But stolen horses were a different
matter, since they traveled faster, and there might be
a delay of some days while the party of horsemen
followed the trail.

Sometimes the Indians skulking on the trail were
more in a warlike frame of mind. In that case, a sleep-
ing guard might be found next morning with one or
more arrows through him and his scalp missing, as
well as the cattle. On occasion, if the guards seemed
inattentive, a mounted band might make a sudden
raid, waving robes and blankets, in an attempt to

stampede the whole herd—and pay special attention
to the saddle horses usually tied near the wagons. If
the trick was successful, and it often was, an outfit
might be left without any way to move the wagons
or even to follow the raiders. In that case there was
nothing to be done except wait for another trail outfit
to come along, in the hope of getting help to recover
at least part of their stolen stock.

If guards were unusually alert, giving the Indians
no chance to steal livestock, the Indians might ride
boldly into camp with much ceremonial handshaking
and many seemingly friendly exclamations of "How!
Friend!" and the like to test the temper of the emi
grants. Besides being bold thieves, they had enor-
mous appetites, especially for coffee, sugar, and white
bread. Men who were experienced in dealing with
Indians kept a firm grip on their weapons and a sharp
watch on any small possessions lying about. After a
proper interval of handshaking and "Hows" the
visitors would be taken to one of the cookfires and all

given coffee with as much sugar as the cooks could spare, then firmly escorted out of camp. Usually they took this treatment philosophically and rode off to wait for an opportunity to steal some livestock later.

But at any sign of timidity on the part of the emigrants the Indians would turn surly and threatening —demanding more and more sugar, reaching into cookpots, rummaging through supply boxes, and making off with clothing, kettles, and anything else that took their fancy. If this brought no strong objection from their victims, they might become progressively more demanding, jerking a gun out of one man's hands, an axe out of another's, or tearing a bit of bright cloth or ribbon from some frightened woman's dress.

Once such a situation had been let to develop, any belated objection might well set off more serious trouble. Often the Indians were gotten rid of only by

a gift of an ox or two for butchering in addition to carrying off what they'd stolen. But having made one such visit, they would usually continue to harass the unfortunate people for days, and their demands become more unreasonable with each succeeding visit.

Even in a strongly guarded camp where the Indians were closely watched, there was usually considerable loss by small pilferage. So in the end there was little to choose between one of the "friendly" visits and the openly hostile harassment.

Besides the Indians, in those days, the plains supported great numbers of antelope, deer, and buffalo besides small game of various kinds. But the emigrants saw few of these creatures, for the constant passing of long lines of creaking wagons, bawling cattle, and shouting men drove wild game to new feeding grounds away from the trail.

Occasionally some hunter riding wide of the wagons would manage to shoot an antelope or a deer. And there were times when the emigrants, finding a river crossing already in use by a herd of migrating buffalo, would get their rifles out of the wagons in the hopes of harvesting some wild beef. But a buffalo, with his high hump and long shaggy mane, was a confusing target and difficult for an inexperienced hunter to bring down, so fresh meat made up a very small part of the emigrants' diet.

Mosquitoes and buffalo gnats, while not exactly game, did live on the plains and probably caused the emigrants more annoyance than all the other wildlife together. From thousands of stagnant pools along the sluggish streams, from pot holes and buffalo wallows on the flats, the mosquitoes rose in clouds. They attacked every inch of exposed flesh and blanketed the hides of horses and cattle, driving them

frantic. The emigrants learned to sit around small smudge fires of green sage whenever possible, but these were of little use to people going about their camp chores. And at night the only escape was to burrow head and all beneath the blankets, not a pleasant solution in hot weather. Sometimes it was necessary to move the camp a mile or two to high ground in order to escape the creatures.

And the buffalo gnats, while smaller, were almost as bad pests. During the day they hung in clouds in front of people's faces, getting into their eyes, nostrils, and ears. They clustered in stinging masses on the tender skin below the dewclaws of the oxen, and in the nostrils of the horses and mules until the animals became unmanageable.

And sometimes, to add variety to the annoyances, the way would lead through country heavily infested by grasshoppers. These did not bite or sting, but

continually flew up from beneath the people's feet and fell into cookpots, skillets, water buckets, and eating utensils. This made eating times somewhat less than a pleasure, especially at night in the dim light of the dying cookfires.

Ordinarily only an occasional solitary buffalo was to be seen along the trail, and beyond the fact that something about the huge dark shaggy shapes sometimes spooked the emigrants' oxen, the buffalo presented no problem. But during their northern migration in the spring they sometimes appeared in herds of thousands, and like oxen, the buffalo had a disconcerting habit of sometimes taking fright and stampeding without apparent reason.

Heads down and tails up they might run blindly for miles in such close-packed masses that the pressure of bodies prevented the leaders from stopping or turning aside from any obstacle in the path. If a string of wagons happened to be caught in the way, many might be overturned, loads scattered, people and teams trampled to death or crippled, and loose stock scattered for miles across the country.

If the column of dust and the rumble of hoofs gave warning in time, the wagons could be pulled into a tight circle and chained together with the livestock inside. From the protection of the wheels on the threatened side, men with rifles fired into the middle of the herd, and as buffalo were killed, others crowded by the ones behind fell over the bodies and were themselves trampled until a barrier had been formed that split the herd so that it flowed by on either side.

Few Prairie Schooner trains were ever caught in such stampedes, but even the possibility did little to endear the buffalo to the emigrants.

CHAPTER NINE

Housekeeping,

Quarrels, and Parties

During the long slow months on the Trail a train of Prairie Schooners was really a moving village, carrying with it most of the problems and small annoyances of village living in addition to the new ones provided by the road itself.

The women still visited neighbors, when time allowed, for a bit of gossip or to borrow a cup of this or that. And even though they had exchanged weathertight houses for wagons covered with flimsy canvas, and familiar kitchens for smoky outdoor cookfires, they still had their families to feed and regular household chores to attend to.

Whenever the wagons halted, bread had to be baked and meat and beans set to cook, no matter how much gritty dust sifted into the mixing bowls and cook pots. Small children had to be dressed, undressed, warned against wandering out onto the prairie, or forbidden to play with the children from the Tennessee wagons.

And, as at home, there were always clothes to be washed and mending and darning to be done. As the big wash pots steamed, there were constant loud and bitter complaints about water so impregnated with minerals that even their harsh homemade soap would not make a suds—or so heavy with river silt that a dusty residue had to be shaken from the clothes after they'd dried.

Housekeeping was difficult enough in dry weather but if a layover was due to rain, conditions grew even worse. Cooking and baking still had to be

done, but to keep a steady heat under kettles and Dutch ovens with oily greasewood or damp buffalo chips was a strain on the most even disposition. And if in desperation a woman had someone arrange a canvas fly to keep the rain off her fire, the stinging acrid smoke would hang underneath, inflaming her eyes and giving her hair and clothing a gamy tang that would last for days.

There were no windows to wash in a Prairie Schooner, nor any floors to scrub, but mold quickly formed on old bread and slabs of salt meat and had to be scraped off. Damp bedding had to be aired somehow and shaken at least partly free from mud and sand, and muddy boots scraped and stuffed with grass.

And often in addition to her other rainy day problems the harassed housewife had to settle quarrels and improvise entertainment for a pack of small children confined to the dark interior of the wagon by the rain. So, taking one thing with another, it is small

wonder that many an otherwise sweet nature was completely soured before the trip was over.

And good weather or bad, when any group of people are thrown closely together for weeks or months, there are certain to be arguments and disputes among neighbors.

There were no courts to appeal to, but nonetheless tempers grew short under the hardships of the trail and such quarrels and misunderstandings could not safely be left to grow into larger troubles. So in almost every train there were men whose opinions and judgment had come to be respected, who heard such grievances and tried to work out solutions acceptable to both sides. These men had no authority to enforce any decision they might make, but they usually had the support of the greater part of the people, and so did in effect serve as a court.

In this way most of the small troubles were ironed out and peace kept in the party, but there were other disagreements that were more difficult to solve. It occasionally happened that there was widespread dissatisfaction with the leadership and conduct of the wagon train itself. And heated arguments could arise over road forks and short cuts in the trail—some wanting to take one way and some the other.

In such circumstances feelings might run so high that the discontented would pull their wagons out of the line and strike out on their own.

But in spite of the hardships, the squabbles, and the housekeeping problems the emigrants found time for parties, also. They were always ready for anything to break the monotony of the trail, and it took no more than the sight of some gaffer hauling a banjo or a fiddle out of his wagon after supper to draw a crowd ready for a fandango. The fact that they danced their reels and formed their figures on dusty buffalo grass was no discouragement. They whirled, bowed, stomped, clapped hands, sang and shouted. And when they were winded, they sat around the smoky fires swatting mosquitoes and telling stories.

The sight must truly have amazed any Indian who happened to be skulking in the darkness beyond the ring of wagons.

CHAPTER TEN

End of the Trail

At the Western edge of the plains the Prairie Schooners took a narrowing way leading into the Rocky Mountains. Leaving the Platte at the North Fork they followed the Sweetwater to the edge of a gently rising plateau that led them through South Pass and across the Continental Divide.

Once on the Western Slope, the trail followed the Big Sandy down to the crossing of Green River and on to Ft. Bridger. From there the route crossed deserts and more mountains and passed Bear River and Soda Springs before coming at last to the Snake. After

the start of the gold rush to California the wagons
of the Forty-niners followed the Oregon Trail as far
as Bear River or Soda Springs. There they branched
off to follow the Humbolt southward to California,
while the Oregon settlers continued up the Snake
past Ft. Boise and over the mountains to the Columbia River valley.

And every mile of the trail continued to bring its
own difficulties. Now, instead of the threat of mud
and quicksand at river crossings, the emigrants had
to deal with swift-flowing streams whose currents
could dash wagons against huge rocks, spilling loads
and breaking wheels and causing great damage to
running gear. They met increasingly steep slopes,
often of slippery rock, where wagons were pulled

slowly up one at a time by doubled or tripled teams. On equally steep downhill slopes the wagons had to be held back by ropes snubbed around trees to prevent them overrunning the teams.

As the road narrowed the grazing became more and more scant so that oxen already weakened by months on the trail sometimes simply lay down and quit in the middle of a long pull. In such a case, if the wheels could not be blocked in time, the heavily loaded wagon might roll backward over a cliff and crash on the rocks below—dragging the teams, still hooked to their chains, along with it.

Each morning it became more difficult to get the weakened cattle to their feet, and for years after the trail was abandoned the way was plainly marked by whitening bones of the hundreds of horses and oxen that had died of accident, lack of feed, or from poisoned water.

As the teams weakened or wagons broke down, the emigrants adjusted their loads to meet the emergency.

A wagon with a broken wheel might be turned into a two-wheeled cart, making the rest of the trip behind two to four pairs of weakened oxen. Others finally abandoned their wagons entirely, packing what remained of their belongings on the backs of their remaining animals.

But in either case, the change meant that more treasured possessions joined the rusting cookstoves, mirrors, broken chains, rocking chairs, tables, and dead animals already littering the edges of the trail. Later in the season cold rain, and even ice and snow, added to their difficulties. But somehow or other the emigrants solved each problem as it appeared and went on.

The wagon trains didn't always arrive in the same order in which they'd started. Some made the trip in three months or a little more, and passed slower outfits on the way. Others, delayed by Indian attack, accident, or through having gotten lost while attempting a short cut across unmapped country, might spend five or six months on the way. Occasionally people died on the way from disease, or were killed by accident or Indians—but babies were born on the trail, also, so the number of people starting the trip and the number arriving in Oregon tended to balance out pretty well.

Year after year the wagons continued to stream west with the numbers on the trail increasing every year, until at last the first transcontinental railroad was built.

But railroads, being profitmaking organizations, would never have made the expensive crossing of the plains and mountains if the Northwest had still been uninhabited. So it was the Prairie Schooner in its thousands, carrying the emigrants to settle the rich Oregon Territory, that was mainly responsible for the moving of the nation's western border from the Missouri to the Pacific Ocean.

Glen Rounds was born in a sod house in the South Dakota Badlands and moved with his family to a ranch in Montana when he was a year old. He says: "My father told me about the trip from South Dakota to Montana. We went in covered wagons, taking 23 days to go 200 miles because of getting the wagons mired in gumbo." He has "prowled the country" as mule skinner, cowpuncher, baker, logger, lightning artist, carnival talker, and sign painter.